W/P

haverfordtownship
free library

1601 Darby Road
Havertown, PA 19083
610-446-3082

library@haverfordlibrary.org
www.haverfordlibrary.org

Your receipt lists your
materials and due dates

Online renewals at
www.haverfordlibrary.org

EARTH DAY
FROM THE
BLACK LAGOON®

Get more monster-sized laughs from

The Black Lagoon®

SET 1 • 6 HARDCOVER BOOKS	**978-1-59961-809-8**
The Class Election from the Black Lagoon	978-1-59961-810-4
The Class Trip from the Black Lagoon	978-1-59961-811-1
The Field Day from the Black Lagoon	978-1-59961-812-8
The Little League Team from the Black Lagoon	978-1-59961-813-5
The Science Fair from the Black Lagoon	978-1-59961-814-2
The Talent Show from the Black Lagoon	978-1-59961-815-9
SET 2 • 6 HARDCOVER BOOKS	**978-1-59961-958-3**
April Fools' Day from the Black Lagoon	978-1-59961-959-0
The Author Visit from the Black Lagoon	978-1-59961-960-6
Back-to-School Fright from the Black Lagoon	978-1-59961-961-3
The School Carnival from the Black Lagoon	978-1-59961-962-0
The Spring Dance from the Black Lagoon	978-1-59961-963-7
The Summer Vacation from the Black Lagoon	978-1-59961-964-4
SET 3 • 9 HARDCOVER BOOKS	**978-1-61479-200-0**
The 100th Day of School from the Black Lagoon	978-1-61479-201-7
The Christmas Party from the Black Lagoon	978-1-61479-202-4
The Halloween Party from the Black Lagoon	978-1-61479-203-1
The New Year's Eve Sleepover from the Black Lagoon	978-1-61479-204-8
The School Play from the Black Lagoon	978-1-61479-205-5
The Snow Day from the Black Lagoon	978-1-61479-206-2
St. Patrick's Day from the Black Lagoon	978-1-61479-207-9
The Thanksgiving Day from the Black Lagoon	978-1-61479-208-6
Valentine's Day from the Black Lagoon	978-1-61479-209-3
SET 4 • 10 HARDCOVER BOOKS	**978-1-61479-599-5**
The Amusement Park from the Black Lagoon	978-1-61479-600-8
The Big Game from the Black Lagoon	978-1-61479-601-5
The Class Picture Day from the Black Lagoon	978-1-61479-602-2
Earth Day from the Black Lagoon	978-1-61479-603-9
Friday the 13th from the Black Lagoon	978-1-61479-604-6
Groundhog Day from the Black Lagoon	978-1-61479-605-3
The Reading Challenge from the Black Lagoon	978-1-61479-606-0
The Secret Santa from the Black Lagoon	978-1-61479-607-7
The Summer Camp from the Black Lagoon	978-1-61479-608-4
Trick or Treat from the Black Lagoon	978-1-61479-609-1

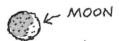

MOON

CHOCOLATE-CHIP COOKIE

EARTH DAY
FROM THE
BLACK LAGOON®

I NEED A PIT STOP.

by Mike Thaler
Illustrated by Jared Lee

SCHOLASTIC INC.

ABDO
Spotlight

For Jared: 30 years—the best! —M.T.

To Jack and June Schneider —J.L.

← SPACE SNAKE

ABDOPUBLISHING.COM

Reinforced library bound edition published in 2017 by Spotlight, a division of ABDO, PO Box 398166, Minneapolis, Minnesota 55439. Spotlight produces high-quality reinforced library bound editions for schools and libraries.
REPRINTED BY PERMISSION OF SCHOLASTIC INC.

Printed in the United States of America, North Mankato, Minnesota.
092016
012017

THIS BOOK CONTAINS RECYCLED MATERIALS

ISBN 978-0-545-47669-0

Text copyright © 2013 by Mike Thaler
Illustrations copyright © 2013 by Jared D. Lee Studio, Inc.

LIBRARY OF CONGRESS CATALOGING-IN-PUBLICATION DATA

This book was previously cataloged with the following information:

Thaler, Mike, 1936-
  Earth Day from the Black Lagoon / by Mike Thaler ; illustrated by Jared Lee.
  p. cm. -- (Black Lagoon adventures; #23)
  Summary: There's an Earth Day celebration in store for Mrs. Green's class, and her students are working on important reports.
  [1. Pollution--Juvenile fiction. 2. Schools--Juvenile fiction. 3. Earth Day--Juvenile fiction.]
I. Title. II Series.
  PZ7.T3 Ear 2013
  [E]--dc23
                    2012286554

978-1-61479-603-9 (reinforced library bound edition)

← PLASTIC SKULL

Spotlight
A Division of ABDO
abdopublishing.com

 ← STAR

CONTENTS

Chapter 1: Green for Green 7

Chapter 2: Read It and Weep 13

Chapter 3: Every Litter Bit Hurts 16

Chapter 4: The New Hubie 20

Chapter 5: No News Is Bad News 22

Chapter 6: Hubie the Re-cyclone 26

Chapter 7: Dream Clouds 30

Chapter 8: The Re-cyclops 34

Chapter 9: Off the Deep End 38

Chapter 10: Recycle Man 40

Chapter 11: Presents of Mind 44

Chapter 12: Earth Mirth 46

Chapter 13: For Mother Earth 51

Chapter 14: Actions Speak as Loud as Words 54

Eric's Ecology Riddles 58

 ← PLANET

CHAPTER 1
GREEN FOR GREEN

When Mrs. Green announced that in two weeks we would celebrate Earth Day, everyone was very excited. Then when she said in preparation we would all have to do reports on special topics, everyone sighed.

She wrote a long list on the board. At least we could choose our topic.

Eric took *endangered species* because he felt class clowns were an endangered species.

Freddy took *food supply*, a subject close to his heart.

Derek took *recycling* because he thought it was about bike riding.

I'VE ALWAYS WANTED TO RIDE A UNICYCLE.

Randy took *global warming* because he thought it was a hot topic.

THE ARCTIC OCEAN IS AS WARM AS BATHWATER.

Doris took *air pollution*, even though she thought it was un-ladylike.

Penny took *solutions* because she's a show-off.

And I was left with *water pollution*.

Eric snickered, "Looks like you're all wet, Hubie!"

CHAPTER 2
READ IT AND WEEP

Next, we all went to the library to do research. We looked in the nonfiction section because all these problems are very real!

SPACE PET →

I felt bad when I read how so many of our rivers, lakes, and even our oceans have been poisoned by pollution. We were all upset on the bus ride home that day.

CHAPTER 3
EVERY LITTER BIT HURTS

CALM DOWN.

"Don't grown-ups care, Mom, what kind of world they're leaving us kids?"

RECYCLED BONE

"It's not just grown-ups, Hubie, it's everyone. When you run the water as you're brushing your teeth, that's wasteful. When you throw a soda can in the regular trash, that's wasteful. When you throw paper on the ground, that's pollution. It all adds up."

"You're right, Mom. I'm going to turn over a new leaf . . . a green leaf."

NEW LEAF

EXACT SIZE

THIS MEANS HUBIE IS GOING TO START BEHAVING IN A BETTER WAY.

18

I'M GOING TO RECYCLE MY BOOGERS.

CHAPTER 4
THE NEW HUBIE

Hubie started by cleaning up his room. Then he went outside and swept up his whole street. He started one recycling bin for aluminum and plastic, one for glass, and one for paper. The world felt better already.

BE BACK FOR DINNER.

OK.

TOXIC
RAIN →

CHAPTER 5
NO NEWS IS BAD NEWS

The next day, everyone gave their reports. Hubie learned a lot. There are places where the tallest mountains are made of garbage.

In the ocean, there are giant islands made of plastic. Soon all the rivers, streams, and lakes will be polluted, and even the rain will be toxic. In years to come there may not be enough food for everyone. And what there is could be poisoned.

DOG
WORM

23

Just then the lunch bell rang, and everyone rushed off to lunch, laughing. Everyone except Hubie. He was the only one who took it seriously.

UNICYCLE →

CHAPTER 6
HUBIE THE
RE-CYCLONE

The new, recycled Hubie stood in the cafeteria line.

"Only take what you're going to eat," he told the kids standing in front of him. "Finish everything you take," he told the kids standing behind him.

WHO MADE YOU THE FOOD COP?

No one listened.

When lunch was finished, there were still mounds of unfinished food left on the plates. So Hubie brought out his secret weapon: Freddy.

I LOVE LEFTOVERS.

Freddy finished everything and licked the plates.

"Waste not, want not," said Hubie.

YUMMY!

CHAPTER 7
DREAM CLOUDS

That night, Hubie had a nightmare. He woke up and the sky was dark. Big clouds of smoke covered the sun. He got dressed and went out to climb a tree, but he couldn't find one.

I'M BORED.

I CAN ALWAYS EAT YOU.

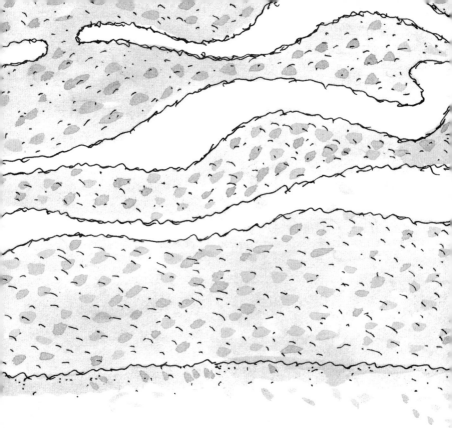

There weren't any flowers, either. In fact, there was nothing green to be seen. The ground was as gray as the sky, and there was no difference between night and day.

MIKE THALER
HAVING A
GLOOMY DAY →

31

He woke up and ran to the window. The sun was just coming up and its light began to warm

the earth. All the flowers turned to welcome it, and the birds sang their thanks for a brand-new day.

CHAPTER 8

THE RE-CYCLOPS

The next day in class, Hubie was even more dedicated.

"Don't put your gum under your desk!" he told Penny.

BUT I'M DONE CHEWING IT.

THAT'S DISGUSTING!

I LOVE GUM.

"Don't waste that piece of paper," he told Eric.

"Recycle your eraser crumbs," he told Derek.

He opened all the windows. He turned off all the lights. He even told Mrs. Green not to give so much homework because everyone would have to stay up late and use lots of electricity.

It was clear that they had created a Re-cyclops monster.

CHAPTER 9
OFF THE DEEP END

At home, Hubie was even worse. He put a sail on the car. He hooked up a lightbulb to the hamster wheel. He wouldn't take a bath Friday night because it would waste water. He even thought about taking the aluminum siding off their house to recycle it. Hubie was going to save the world. He felt like a superhero!

39

CHAPTER 10
RECYCLE MAN

Faster than a rolling aluminum can.

Able to leap piles of garbage in a single bound.

It's a word.
It's a plan.
It's Recycle Man.

A group of unthinking school kids are about to drop their ice-cream wrappers on the ground, but before they can, Recycle Man brings in a garbage can.

"The can can," he tells them, "make a cleaner, healthier, safer environment."

41

"Hubie, wake up! We're at school," says T-Rex.

"Huh, huh, oh. T-Rex, turn off the engine. You're wasting gas and polluting the air!"

42

CHAPTER 11
PRESENTS OF MIND

"Well, class, tomorrow is Earth Day, and I'd like you each to bring in a present for Mother Earth," announced Mrs. Green.

Everybody scratched their head. Hubie took out a pencil and started writing.

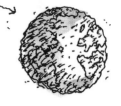

CHAPTER 12
EARTH MIRTH

It was Friday, and everyone was very excited.

Doris did a dance for Mother Earth.

WHAT GRACE.

WHAT FORM.

I'M SO MOVED.

OH, BROTHER.

46

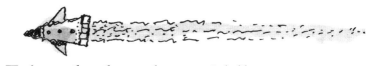

Eric asked ecology riddles.*

MAY I HAVE YOUR UNDIVIDED ATTENTION?

*SEE PAGE 58

Randy made a wastebasket out of a large tin can.

"It's your turn, Hubie," said Mrs. Green.

COUGH, COUGH.

RELAX.

TAKE A DEEP BREATH.

Hubie stepped to the front of the class and cleared his throat. "A poem," he announced.

← DOG ALLERGIC TO FROGS

49

A FEW EARTH FACTS

THE WORD "EARTH" COMES FROM ENGLISH AND GERMAN WORDS THAT MEAN "GROUND."

EARTH IS THE ONLY PLANET NOT NAMED AFTER A ROMAN OR GREEK GOD.

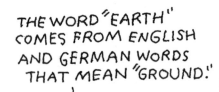

EARTH HAS ONE MOON.

THERE ARE 7 BILLION PEOPLE LIVING ON EARTH.

EARTH IS THE FIFTH-LARGEST PLANET IN THE SOLAR SYSTEM.

EARTH IS AROUND 4.6 BILLION YEARS OLD.

CHAPTER 13
FOR MOTHER EARTH

← SNACK

Dear Earth Mother,
You are so great.
We have no other.
You give us everything we
    need,
But we need to take heed.

WOULD YOU LIKE A RIDE?

NO, THANKS, I'LL JUST KEEP ON ROLLING.

If we are careless with
  pollution,
We will be airless, with no
  solution.
If we are sloppy with our waste,
Our water will have a funny
  taste.
Unless we have more car pools,
We will run out of fuels.
We all need to take more care,
So when we grow up
You'll still be there.

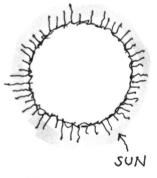

SUN

THE SUN IS
93 MILLION
MILES
FROM
EARTH.

EARTH

IN THE MIDDLE AGES, PEOPLE THOUGHT THE EARTH WAS FLAT.
CAPTAIN, WE NEED TO TURN BACK!
JUST A LITTLE FARTHER.
STAY SAFE!
SEA
LAND
EARTH
FIRE-BREATHING DRAGONS WAIT FOR THE NEXT SHIP TO FALL OFF THE FACE OF THE EARTH.

CHAPTER 14
ACTIONS SPEAK AS LOUD AS WORDS

Everyone sat with their mouths open as Hubie sat down.

Then, one by one, they started to applaud till the whole class was standing up and cheering.

"Well," said Hubie, "let's all go out and pick up trash."
And they did.

56

And that's how they celebrated
Earth Day!

ERIC'S ECOLOGY RIDDLES

1. When is the earth sad?
When it's down in the dumps.

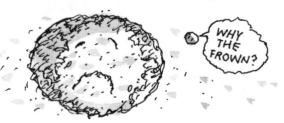

2. What do you call it when the air is filled with rabbits?
Hare pollution.

3. When is a boat cheapest to buy?
When it's on sail.

4. What do you call a sun-powered tooth?

A solar molar.

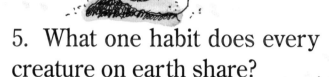

5. What one habit does every creature on earth share?

Our habit-tat.

6. What nation can change the world?

Your imagi-nation.

HMMM.

7. What race is everyone in?
The human race.

8. Where do you mail organic garbage?
At the compost office.

9. What three letters run everything?
N R G.

10. What is recycling?
A pollution solution.

11. Why was Doctor Frankenstein an environmentalist?
Because he made his monster from recycled parts.

12. How can the earth get in shape?
By reducing its waist.

13. What ability does everyone on earth have to help the environment?
Response-ability.

14. What kind of vehicle can we all ride to a better life?
A re-cycle.

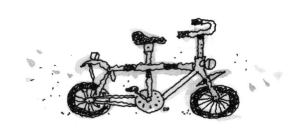

15. "Knock, knock."
"Who's there?"
"Trash can."
"Trash can who?"
"Trash can ruin the world."

16. "Knock, knock."
"Who's there?"
"Garden."
"Garden who?"
"Garden the environment is important."

And remember—to save our planet, plan it!

WE CAN ALL PITCH IN.